OnE

A Day Like Any Other

Gormy's day started much like any other.
He woke up thinking about monstering
(after a whole night dreaming about
monstering), and decided that today was
the day that he was going to become the
most monstrous monster ever.

He jumped out of bed, stretched his tail
and straightened his pointy blue ears. Then

he measured his one, quite good fang with a piece of string to check whether it had grown (it hadn't).

Gormy scampered downstairs, eventually arriving at the bottom (monstrous stairs are tremendously long) to the

SpOrp!

GLotch!

SpoOoorp

of his mother mincing a cow for cow jam.

Gormy's mother, Mogra, was a monster of the hairy, pink variety. She was ten times hairier and pinker than any animal you could imagine and was so big that Gormy could hide between her toes.

"I hope you're hungry, Gormy – the jam's almost ready," said Mogra. Gormy licked his lips in delight (being careful not to cut himself on his fang). As he clambered eagerly up an enormous chair leg to the table, he noticed his father by the window.

Grumbor was even bigger than Mogra, and had so many horns and tusks that hugging him was actually dangerous. He was staring intently into the garden.

"What are you looking at, Dad?" said Gormy.

"There's something out here that I think you should see," said Grumbor in a voice so rumbling that it made the jam curdle.

"What is it?" said Gormy. Grumbor's
huge hand swept down and scooped Gormy
up to the window. Gormy looked out.

"Snow!" he cried in astonishment.

Sure enough, the whole
garden was covered in a
thick layer of bright,
white snow. It was
everywhere, from
the lawn to the top
of the
hedges, to
the tip of
the Very
Tall Tree.
Even Gormy's
treehouse, which nestled in the Very Tall
Tree's highest branches, was covered.

"Lovely, isn't it? We haven't had snow in

4

Octobuary for years," said Gormy's mother, dipping one of her massive claws into the jam and tasting it. "Needs more cow," she added to herself.

"Can we go outside and play?" asked Gormy, beside himself with excitement.

"Play?" laughed his father, raising two of his eyebrows. "Why would you want to play when you can *monster*? After breakfast, I want you to fetch your **How to be a Better Monster** book, then meet me in the garden for Lesson Six Hundred and Fivety-Seven: Know Your Snow."

A lesson about snow? thought Gormy. *What does snow have to do with monstering?* Never had two more exciting things gone together! Well, not since he tried eating donkey and horse at the same time. Gormy swallowed his breakfast without chewing, and after four or five appreciative burps, he rushed into his bedroom to get his **How to be a Better Monster** book.

TWO

KnOW Your Snow

Gormy opened his Big Chest of Monstrously Excellent Things. He rummaged past a fishing rock, a pack of trouble-gum and two bags of boom-balloons, before taking out his **How to be a Better Monster** book. He hurried downstairs into the kitchen, and opened the back door. He was met with a nose-full of biting cold air.

"Finally! I thought you'd never open the door!" said a small, gruff voice. Gormy looked down to see Mike the scuttybug, shivering on the doorstep.

Mike was about as horrid as monstrous beetles get. He ticked every box when it came to ugliness, sliminess and ugly-related sliminess. But he was Gormy's only real friend, and if you ignored the smell, he was really quite nice.

"Mike! Are you all right?" said Gormy, dusting the snow off Mike's back with a furry finger.

"Of course I'm not all right! It's freezing out here!" grumbled the scuttybug.

"Do you want to come inside? I think my dad's just been to the toilet. . ."

"Fresh dung! Great! That'll warm me up," said Mike, happily scuttying inside.

Gormy made his way into the garden. He looked for his father, but he was nowhere to be seen. He thought about waiting patiently, but not for very long. The sight of all that unspoiled snow was just too tempting to resist – Gormy leapt straight in!

FWUMP!

It was even thicker than Gormy had imagined! He was almost up to his belly buttons in it (all three of them!). The freezing snow clung to his fur and sent shivers down his tail. He leapt into the air again, bouncing around like a happy Hop-gobbin.

PwOmp! FOmp! Pwump!

It was then he noticed a large, round mound of snow. It looked perfect for jumping into! Gormy bounded towards it. He took a deep, cold breath, and leapt!

GReEoOAArgghH!

The mound exploded! Gormy's father

appeared, roaring and looking like he was about to swallow Gormy whole.

Gormy screamed and bounced off his father's nose. He landed with a **FLOMP!** in the snow. He was still shaking when Grumbor reached into the snow and pulled him out.

"The key to winter monstering," said Grumbor, as he put Gormy back on his feet, "is to know your snow."

Gormy looked at the place where Grumbor had appeared from. There was a massive, Grumbor-sized hole in the ground. He had dug a hiding place and covered himself with snow . . . just to scare the fur off Gormy!

"Snow may seem like a lot of fun, but for a monster it can mean the difference between scaring and being scared. Knowing your snow will make you a better monster."

"A better monster," echoed an excited Gormy.

"Good. Now look behind you. What do you see?" said Grumbor.

Gormy looked back. It wasn't a difficult question to answer. Even the house was covered.

"Snow?" he answered.

"Here, in the snow – your *tracks*. Anyone can tell where you have been. That is why monsters have tails – to brush the snow behind us, so that no one can tell where we've gone or where we're going. That is how I was able to surprise you. That is how you will become a monster. Not like hoomums. All they do with snow is play in it and throw snowballs and build snowhoomums. It isn't monstrous at all."

Actually, that sounds like quite a lot of fun, thought Gormy, but he decided not to say anything. The next moment, his mother appeared at the back door.

"That's enough monstering for today!

The monstersitter will be here any minute," she called. Gormy's pointy blue ears pricked up in horror.

"Monstersitter? Why is a monstersitter coming?" he said, panicking. Being monstersat (which is like being babysat but less predictable) was terribly unmonstrous. In fact, it was only slightly less unmonstrous than the three most unmonstrous things of all – talking to a hoomum, being a vegetarian, and (worst of all) having a nightmare!

"Great gobs! I completely forgot!" said Grumbor, slapping a huge, clawed hand against his forehead. "Our monsterversary!"

"Monsterversary? What's a monsterversary?" said Gormy.

"Our wedding monsterversary! Tomorrow, your mother and I will have been married for fivety-two and nine-ninetieths! We're going away for the night, so we got you a monstersitter," said Grumbor, tramping back to the house.

"I don't need a monstersitter!" protested Gormy, but his cries were drowned out by the

Krunch! **G**runch!

of his father's footsteps. Gormy's day had just gone from brilliantly monstrous to about as bad as bad days get.

15

Three

Nana the noog

Gormy tramped sulkily back to the house. He had barely had time to brush the snow off his fur when the doorbell sneezed.

"There's the monstersitter now! Be a good little puffball and answer the door," called Gormy's mother from upstairs.

Gormy dragged his feet all the way to the front door, wondering which of the monstersitters it would be. Not surprisingly, it was hard to find anyone to even go near a house full of monsters. Even other monsters were worried Grumbor would stomp on them just for the sake of it. This meant that the monstersitters that did venture to Peatree Hill were particularly strange. They included:

DRUMP THE DUMP – a perfectly pleasant ogre from the next valley. Drump the Drump smelled so unspeakably dreadful that it made Gormy vomit every time he came near. The house reeked of Drump and monster sick for months afterwards.

YELLOWSOCKS – a tree-gnome with an annoyingly long beard. The main trouble with Yellowsocks was that he was allergic to monsters. He started sneezing the second he saw Gormy, and didn't stop until Grumbor "accidentally" stepped on him.

OLD SPRIGGLE – some sort of cross between a witch and a goblin. Old Spriggle was one of the meanest creatures in the valley. She would only monstersit on the condition that Gormy sang to her constantly.

I bet it'll be someone even worse, thought Gormy. He sighed and opened the door.

"BOO!"

A strange creature leapt out in front of Gormy! He screamed for the second time that morning, and jumped so high with fright that his horns hit the ceiling (and monstrous ceilings are very high).

"Got you, didn't I?" said the strange creature. Gormy took a good look at her. She was about as big as a fat hoomum, with huge, bat-like ears and wrinkly, yellowy-green skin. She wore a cloak of rags (that must have been knitted together in the dark) and had a rather odd clump of red

hair, which sat on her head like a bad hat.

"I am a noog, but since noogs have no name, you can call me Nana. And what's your name, little monster?"

"Gormy Ruckles," said Gormy.

"Noog's alive, what a scary name! You must be the most monstrously monstrous monsterboy I've ever met! And look at that fang – you could bite off a yobbin's head with that. In fact, you could bite off all four of them!" said Nana the noog.

Gormy was delighted! He had wanted someone to call him monstrous for as long as he could remember (which was precisely as long as he'd had a tail. Monsters can't remember much of anything until their tail grows. Monsters who lose their tails often forget how to be monstrous, and must retrain or take early retirement).

"Such impressive monstrousness deserves a reward," continued Nana the noog. She twirled a fat finger, and in a pop of colour, a shiny, yellow sweet appeared in her hand. "Here!"

"Thanks!" said Gormy. He took the sweet and popped it eagerly into his mouth. But the moment he swallowed it, *POP!* he turned completely yellow!

"Hee hee! You've been nooged!" laughed Nana.

"How did you do that?" said Gormy, staring in amazement at his yellow paws.

"Just a little old-fashioned magic! It's easy when you know how – and Nana knows best!" said Nana.

Gormy couldn't believe it – real magic! Things were turning out much better than he had expected!

"Better put you back to normal before your parents notice," said Nana with a wink. Then, with a twirl of her finger,

Gormy was blue again! He tried not to giggle as (one-and-a-half seconds later) Mogra and Grumbor came downstairs.

"Well, it's nice to see you're getting on so well," said Mogra. "You must be the monstersitter?"

"She's a noog, but since noogs have no name, you can call her Nana," said Gormy, suddenly rather excited about being monstersat.

"Well, Nana, I can't thank you enough for agreeing to monstersit. You're the only monstersitter still advertising in the

Monster Gazette," said Mogra.

"Oh, I love monstersitting – you never know what's going to happen!" said Nana.

"Well, it's time we were off," said Grumbor. "We need to be at the Bog of Horror cave-spa by two o'clock – your mother's having a wasp's nest facial."

Mogra leaned all the way down to Gormy. She opened her huge, pink claw to reveal a small shiny object, tied to a piece of string. She hung it around Gormy's neck. "This is a pinch-bell. If there are any problems, any problems at all, give this a squeeze, and we'll come running," she said.

Pinch-bells are sort of like long-distance, monstrous alarms. They come in two halves – one containing the top half of a fairy, the other the bottom. Squeezing the bottom half makes the top half squeal, no

matter how far away the halves are.
Squeezing the top half isn't recommended,
as fairy farts smell surprisingly nasty.

"There's
nothing to worry
your horns
about. I'll take
good care of your
little monster,"
said Nana.

Moments later,
Gormy watched his parents tramp off into
the snow and disappear behind Peatree
Hill. Nana the noog closed the door and
grinned a wide grin.

"I thought they'd never leave! Let the
games begin – race you to the garden!" she
cried.

Four

Noog Games

Gormy quickly realized that Nana wasn't
at all like his other monstersitters. He'd
never known anyone who liked to play as
much as she did! They began with a
snowball fight – but this was a particularly
noogish snowball fight. Every time Nana
threw a snowball, she twirled her finger and,
POP!, it was transformed! One

second it was a snowball and the next it was:

A ROCK

(which hit Gormy on the head. As soon as he
woke up, he shouted, "That was brilliant!" and
immediately made Nana do it again)

A FIREBALL

(which set Gormy's tail alight. He was still
giggling long after the fire was put out)

A LIVE RABBIT

(which, once caught, served as a
delicious mid-game snack)

Next, they set to work building a snowmonster (which was like a snowhoomum
but eleventy times more monstrous).

"It's not exactly scary, is it?" said Gormy,
trying his best to fashion claws out of dry
twigs.

"I know how we can make it *really* monstrous," said Nana the noog. Then she twirled her finger and,

the snowmonster was transformed. It looked exactly like Gormy!

"It's a snow . . . me!" said Gormy, admiring his image. Then he turned to Nana and said, "Do you really think I'm monstrous?"

"Are you kidding? You're *so* monstrous

I'm surprised you haven't tried to eat me yet!" said Nana. No one had ever said anything so nice to him!

Gormy swelled with pride. He had completely forgotten why he hated being monstersat. He didn't even mind that his parents had gone to the land beyond the hill without him. He took the pinch-bell from around his neck and placed it on the snow-Gormy.

"There, now it really looks like me!" he giggled.

For the rest of the day, Gormy and Nana tore around the garden (being careful not to fall in the enormous hole that his father had dug!) playing so many games that you'd need to be a fivety-fingered flummock just to keep count. However, these were no ordinary, monster games like *Stomp on the Village* or *Roar at That!* These were *noog* games, so noogishly noogiful in their noogishness that they were impossible to describe without using the word 'noog'. Each game was packed with more magic than Gormy could have wished for. By the time the sun slipped behind the Very Tall Tree, Gormy was sure that this was the best day *ever*.

"Noog's alive, aren't you tired yet? You've got more energy than any monster I've ever met! I'm not sure I've got it in me to play Noog-in-the-Middle. . ."

"Noog-in-the-Middle! How do you play that?" asked Gormy, excitedly.

"Right then, first you take three big spoons and an old curtain. Then we do a bit of good, old-fashioned finger-twirling and—"

Nana stopped. She stared into the sky, open-mouthed. The sun had all but disappeared behind the trees, and it was getting dark.

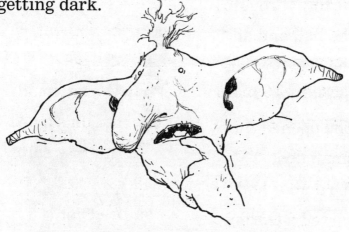

"And then what?" said Gormy, with monstrous anticipation.

"Is it that time already? Noog's alive,

where has the day gone? It's time for bed!"
Nana rushed back into the house as if her
feet were on fire.

"Already? But I don't go to bed until the
moon is higher than the Very Tall Tree!"
began Gormy, chasing Nana into the kitchen.

"A growing monster needs his sleep.
Nana knows best!" said Nana. She hurried
Gormy through
the hall and all
the way upstairs
to his bedroom.
She opened the
small door
(Grumbor had
carved a Gormy-
sized door out of

the monstrously big door to make it easier
for Gormy to open) and nudged him inside.

"Now you must promise me you'll stay in your room until the morning. Don't open this door until the sun rises on the hill, no matter what you hear."

"But—" began Gormy.

"And no sneaking out, mind you. We noogs have terrible eyes but our ears can hear a mouse squeak from one hundred and nine paces. Do you promise?"

"I . . . I promise," sighed Gormy.

"Good boy, and remember, stay in your room! Nana knows best!" said Nana, and shut the door.

What was all that about? We were having so much fun! I knew it couldn't last. . . Ugh, this *is why I hate monstersitters,* thought Gormy. He stared out of the window. In the moonlight he could see new snow falling on the ground. Maybe Nana would let him play in it tomorrow, before his parents got back.

Gormy decided it would be best if he went to sleep, even though he didn't want to. He got into bed, pulled the covers over his head and tried counting sheep to help him nod off (of course, monsters count sheep jumping into a boiling pot).

He had reached three hundred and twenty-eight when he finally fell asleep. . .

Five

Stay in Your Room

Gormy awoke with a start! What was that noise? It sounded like the house was falling in!

He looked around, but it was pitch dark, so he could hardly see anything (most monsters are rubbish at seeing in the dark, despite mostly monstering at night. At least half the destruction caused by a monstrous rampage is due to them accidentally bumping into things).

KRISH!
KOSH!

The noises were coming from downstairs. Had a pack of wolves got into the house? Gormy wasn't at all keen on wolves. He had managed to scare one once, but a whole pack? That was a different matter. Also, where was Nana? Even with all her magic he wasn't sure she could handle all those teeth and claws.

KRUMP!
SMASH!

Gormy remembered his promise to Nana. *Stay in your room . . . no matter what you hear*, she had said. He didn't want to get into trouble. But surely he'd be in more trouble if his monstersitter ended up being mauled to pieces! Plus, curiosity and monster boys go hand-in-claw. Gormy reached for the handle, and opened the door.

KASH!
KOSH!

Gormy tiptoed on to the landing, and started to creep downstairs. He put his hand against the wall to steady himself and felt something jagged and uneven. Gormy could just make out what it was – *claw marks*. They were much bigger than a wolf could make. For a split second he thought it might be something *worse* than wolves. But then, what was worse than wolves?

CRA-TASH!

Downstairs everything was in pieces. The carpet was shredded and the old grandmonster clock lay in pieces on the floor.

The bangs and crashes were coming from the kitchen. Nervously, Gormy inched his way to the kitchen door and poked his head around. Something was rummaging around the pantry, throwing out pots and pans and eating anything it could.

Whatever it was, it was no wolf. It was

HUGE

and Gormy noticed it had a long, spiked tail, stretching out across the floor.

Gormy stared at it for a moment. Then, for no good reason at all, he said, "Hello?"

The creature in the pantry leapt backwards. It was big as Grumbor – no, bigger! It had dark green scales all over its body and dozens of sharp spikes down its back. It was crouched on all fours, with an extra set of arms thrown in for good measure. Its huge, flat head seemed to be made entirely of teeth and green drool. It also had a rather odd clump of red hair, which sat on its head like a bad hat. It looked, quite frankly, *monstrous*.

"Little monster . . ." snarled the monster-like creature,

in a voice nineteen times rougher than sandpaper.

"Excuse me, have you seen Nana?" asked Gormy in his least monstrous whimper.

All of a sudden, the monster burped! A drool-covered ball of dark material flew out of its mouth and landed

SPLOT!

on the floor. It was Nana's cloak. The monster had swallowed it! Which could only mean one thing. . .

"You ate Nana!" cried Gormy.

"Still . . . hungry . . ." said the monster. As Gormy backed away towards the door, it pounced!

"AAaaaaaaahh!"

screamed Gormy as he leapt out of the way!
The monster crashed into the kitchen door,
digging in its claws. It tried to pull away,
but it was stuck! It shook frantically to get
free. Gormy Ruckles took this opportunity
to do something surprisingly
unmonstrous – he ran away as fast as he
could!

Six

The Room of Doom

Gormy bolted upstairs as he heard the kitchen door rip off its hinges! He raced down the landing, and straight into the Room of Doom. Gormy had no idea why it was called the Room of Doom. It was just a big cupboard filled with mops and old boxes. Still, he hoped that the big sign, which read Room of Doom in very

monstrous writing, might be enough to put the monster off.

What am I going to do? The monster ate Nana and now it wants to eat me! thought Gormy. He'd never even heard of a monster-eating monster before (The Most Immense Slood liked to *smell* monsters, but then he did have forty noses).

Gormy sat huddled by the door listening to the monster's thunderous footsteps. With every

FOOOM!

– step –

FOoOM!

– the footsteps –

FOoOM!

– got closer!

Then suddenly, they stopped. There was silence. Gormy waited. And waited. In fact, he waited for what seemed like the whole of Mug'Uggin (the secret month, which likes to hide between March and Junetember). After a while he even got a bit bored.

Maybe the monster went home . . . thought Gormy. It seemed pretty unlikely, but (for the second time that night) curiosity got the better of him. He reached for the handle, and opened the door. . .

"BOO!"

The monster was waiting outside the door! Gormy was now face to face with it, and all he could see were rows and rows of teeth! He darted back into the Room of Doom.

"Still. . . hungry. . ." the monster snarled in a voice that made the paint on the walls start to melt. It squeezed itself into the Room of Doom and moved towards Gormy.

"Leave me alone! Aren't you full yet? You just ate a whole noog!" cried Gormy in desperation. This made the monster laugh so hard that two of its teeth fell out.

"Stupid little monster . . . haven't you worked it out yet?" laughed the monster, twirling one of its claws. "Nana knows best!"

Gormy's two hearts skipped a beat. Suddenly everything made a horrible sort of sense! Nana telling him to stay in his room, the cloak of rags, the clump of hair! The monster didn't eat Nana . . . the monster *was* Nana!

"Nana?" Gormy whimpered. He barely had time to be shocked by the realization – the Nana-monster opened her jaws, revealing twelve rows of sharp, yellow teeth, and moved in for the kill. Gormy closed his eyes. . .

Just then, Gormy heard a loud, creaking sound. He opened an eye and looked down. He was standing on a large, square platform, which looked slightly different to the rest of the floor. As the Nana-monster lunged, the floor disappeared from beneath him!

It was a trap door!

"AAaaaaaaahh!"

screamed Gormy.

As he fell (and fell and fell!) he realized this might be why it was called the Room of Doom. After all, how many trap doors to who-knows-where are there in your cupboard? He was two-thirds of the way through that thought when. . .

KLUD!

. . .he hit the floor!

Seven

To Pinch the Pinch-Bell

Gormy got to his feet and rubbed his head.
A room with a secret trap door – how
brilliantly monstrous! High above him, the
Nana-monster was trying to squeeze herself
through the trap door, but with all of her
enormous monstrousness, she was just too
big. After a few moments, she gave up and
disappeared from sight.

Gormy breathed a sigh of relief. He looked around, but it was so dark he couldn't even see his own nose.

"So, how's that new monstersitter working out? Everything tickety-boo?" said a voice behind him.

"*Mike? Is that you?*" asked Gormy.

"Course it's me! Who else is warming himself up in your cellar?" replied Mike.

"The cellar! So this is where the trap door goes!" said Gormy.

"Yep – although I prefer to use the door – it involves a lot less falling and screaming," said Mike.

"Mike, you've got to help me – it's Nana! The monstersitter has turned into a monster!"

"A monster, eh? Well, at least now you've got something in common," said Mike.

"But she wants to *eat* me! She's a monster-eating monster!" shouted Gormy.

"Hmm, that could be tricky, what with you being a monster and all. I didn't think monsters ate monsters. Why does she want to eat you?"

"How should I know? I didn't hang around to ask!" said Gormy, looking up at the trap door to see if the Nana-monster had come back.

"Oh well, your mum and dad will be back tomorrow. I'm sure they'll know what to do. You'll just have to stay here where it's nice and warm."

"I can't stay in the cellar until tomorrow night! I'll starve!" cried Gormy (monsters had to eat at least five meals a day to maintain even basic levels of monstrousness).

"Well, you could always give them a bell . . . then again, I'm not sure they'll be too happy about your interrupting their monsterversary," suggested Mike.

"The pinch-bell! I forgot all about it!" said Gormy. He reached for it around his neck, but it wasn't there. "Oh no! I put it on the snow-Gormy! It's in the garden!"

"Then it's lucky for you I know my way around this place. Follow me," said Mike.

Gormy followed Mike's voice through the darkness. They clambered over a crate of digestion rocks and a box of his dad's old monstering magazines, then up some stairs to a large door. Gormy pushed it open and climbed out. He was in the back garden! He could hear the Nana-monster had returned to the kitchen – she was loudly smashing or

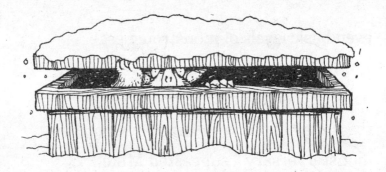

eating whatever she could lay her claws on.

"Stay quiet! She can hear a mouse squeak from one hundred and nine paces!" whispered Gormy. He set about looking for his snowy self, being especially careful not to fall into the giant hole his father had dug. Then, in the moonlight, Gormy spotted something that looked very much like . . . him!

"There it is!" he whispered. He waded through the snow until he reached the snow-Gormy. Sure enough there, around its neck, was the pinch-bell. But as he reached out to grab it. . .

SNAP!

Gormy had trodden on a twig!

"I hear you, little monster!" came a cry.
Gormy turned back to the house, to see the
Nana-monster burst through the kitchen
wall! A shower of bricks, glass, pots, pans
and various other monstrous kitchen-
related things was sent halfway across the
garden! Gormy looked around but there
was nowhere to hide! Then he remembered

how his father had hidden from him earlier that day. He held his breath, and dived into the thick snow!

"Where are you? I know you're there. . ." rumbled the Nana-monster, her hot breath melting the snow around her. She squinted in the darkness. She could see Gormy, frozen to the spot with fear. The Nana-monster bared her claws, and leapt!

SPWAT!

Eight

Escape to the Treehouse

The Nana-monster landed right on top of Gormy, squashing him flat! She laughed a deep, drool-filled laugh, and lifted her foot. But there was nothing there, only snow! She'd squashed the snow-Gormy!

"Where are you, little monster?" she bellowed.

Gormy decided, very wisely, *not* to

answer. He couldn't believe his luck! The
Nana-monster had seen the snow-Gormy,
and mistaken it for him!

With the Nana-monster still roaring in
anger, he dug himself out of his snowy
hiding place, and hurried as quietly as he
could down the garden. As he
moved through the snow,
he carefully covered his
tracks with his tail, just
like his father taught
him. He quickly
reached the
Very Tall Tree
and started to
climb. He
didn't look back until he reached the top.
Once he was safely in his treehouse, he
watched the Nana-monster rampaging

around the garden in search of a Gormy-shaped snack.

"That was close! Glad she only ended up stomping the snow-you – it could have been messy otherwise," whispered Mike.

"I still didn't get the pinch-bell," sighed Gormy. "We'll have to stay up here and keep quiet until she goes back in the house."

"Stay here? We'll freeze!" said Mike.

"Shhh! She'll hear us!" whispered Gormy. He looked around for something to help them keep warm. Stuffed into the corner of the treehouse were:

🐾 ONE HALF-EATEN MOUSECAKE

(which was deliciously rotten but frozen solid)

🐾 ONE DOG-EARED COPY OF

MONSTER BOY'S OWN

(a popular monster comic featuring tales of

daring, adventure and stomping)

 ONE PILE OF SMALL ROCKS

(to throw at passing birds)

 ONE BLANKET

The blanket! He'd forgotten he'd left it there! It had been his favourite since he was just a third-and-a-half (his mother had knitted it from his father's summer shedding). He unrolled it and wrapped it around himself and Mike.

Gormy stared out over the land

beyond the hill. As the sun began to rise he could see the vast, snowy duvet that covered the fields. It was as if a great frosty winderbeast had thrown up over the whole valley – it was the most beautiful thing he had ever seen. He wondered if he would ever get to monster in it.

"Do you think I'll be a real monster one day?" he whispered to Mike.

"Sure! You'll be the most monstrous monster ever! As long as you don't get eaten by your monstersitter, that is," Mike replied.

Gormy looked back. At the other end of the garden, he could see the Nana-monster, still looking for him. She had ripped up every tree in the garden, and all but destroyed the house.

"At least we're safe here – as long as we stay quiet," said Gormy. He sniffed, and wiped a cold, wet droplet from under his nose. It tickled slightly. He rubbed it again, but it just tickled even more.

"Uh-oh," he said.

"What's the matter?" asked Mike.

"I think I'm going to sn . . . sn . . . sn. . ." began Gormy.

"No, don't!" cried Mike.

"Aa-AA-aaa-CHOOO!"

Nine

Treehouse of Terror

Gormy's unfortunately timed sneeze was, in fact, the fourteenth most monstrous sneeze ever heard. It blew all of the snow from the top of the Very Tall Tree, dislodged three pigeons from their perches and scared a sleeping owl to death. And it was more than loud enough to let the Nana-monster know where they were.

"There you are!" she howled, and bounded towards them! Within seconds, she was climbing the Very Tall Tree!

"She's going to eat me! What are we going to do?" yelped Gormy. He grabbed his pile of bird-pelting rocks, and started throwing them at her. But they just bounced off her scaly skin like they were scuttybug droppings. The Nana-monster laughed, and kept on climbing.

"She's nearly at the top – and there's no way out but down! We're trapped up here! Trust me to be a scuttybug and not a scuttyfly!" cried Mike, scuttying frantically around Gormy's head.

"Fly . . . Mike, that's it! You're a genius!"
said Gormy, suddenly having a monstrous
(or monstrously stupid) idea. He grabbed
his blanket by all four corners and held it
behind him. "Hang on, Mike!"

Gormy ran to the edge of the treehouse.
Just as the Nana-monster reached the
top, he jumped! He leapt
over the Nana-monster's
snapping jaws. Mike
held on tightly to
Gormy's fur as they
plummeted downwards.
Then,

PWOOOSH!

The blanket opened like a
parachute! Gormy was
floating through the air!

He soared over the garden, over the hedges, trees and snow-covered lawn. Gormy had never even dreamed of flying (monsters usually dream about roaring, stomping or chomping), but it was monstrously exciting!

If I don't get eaten, I'm definitely going to try this again, he thought. In fact, Gormy was having such a good time that for a second, he forgot all about the Nana-monster.

But only for a second.

"Gormy, she's after us again!" yelled Mike. Gormy turned his head to see the Nana-monster leap out of the tree! She crashed to the ground and immediately started bounding after them and gnashing her jaws. And all the time, Gormy was getting closer to the ground.

"Make us go higher!" shouted Mike.

"I can't! It only goes down!" said Gormy, frantically trying to flap his legs.

"Still hungry!" cried the Nana-monster.

Gormy had almost floated the whole length of the garden. They were almost at the house! As they inched ever closer to the ground, he spotted something glinting in one of the Nana-monster's giant claw-prints.

"The pinch-bell!" he cried. Gormy steered towards it, the snow-crunching sound of the Nana-monster getting ever closer. As they sped towards the ground, Gormy and Mike closed their eyes.

PLOOMP! POMP! KA-FUMP!

Gormy skidded and bounced along the ground like an out of control snowbomb! By the time his brain had stopped rattling, the shadow of the Nana-monster was looming over him.

"Too late, little monster!" roared the Nana-monster and pounced!

GWUMP!

The Nana-monster disappeared into the snow! She was stuck fast in a giant hole – the hiding-hole that Gormy's father had dug the day before!

"The hole . . . she jumped right into it!" said Gormy, as the Nana-monster roared in anger. Gormy didn't waste another second – he grabbed hold of the pinch-bell and squeezed with all his monstrous might!

"I hope your parents heard it," said

Mike, shaking the snow off his antennae.

Then a strange thing happened. As the morning sun shone on to the hole in the ground, the Nana-monster stopped roaring. In fact, she went very quiet indeed. Gormy crept towards the hole.

"Where are you going? That's the way to the monster-eating monster!" said Mike.

But what Gormy saw wasn't a monster-eating monster. In fact, it wasn't a monster at all. It was a plain old noog, looking exactly as she had when Gormy first met her.

"Noog's alive, I've done it again, haven't I?" said Nana.

Ten

The Trouble with noogs

By the time Gormy had helped Nana the noog out of the giant hole, she had apologized a total of thirty-eight times.

"This is the trouble with noogs! We're lovely, magical, noogiful creatures by day, and savage, monster-eating monsters by night. It's just one of those things. . ." explained Nana.

"But how come you've managed to be a monstersitter all this time? You must have eaten every monster boy in the valley," asked Mike.

"All the other little monsters have stayed in their rooms – they've been too tired after a day of noog-games to wake up. And if they do hear me crashing around, they're just too scared to come out. What a brave little monster you must be, Gormy," said Nana.

"I was a little bit scared when you were chasing after me," confessed Gormy, though he tried to sound braver than he felt.

"You won't tell, will you?" begged Nana. "I'd be so lonely without my monstersitting. It's not easy making friends when you turn into a monster-eating monster every night."

Gormy couldn't help feeling sorry
for Nana. Here he was, trying
to be more
monstrous, and she
wanted to be
anything but!

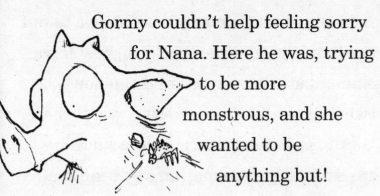

"Don't worry, your secret is safe with us.
Right Mike?"

"Naturally! But I reckon we should fix
the place up before your parents get back,"
said Mike.

"My parents! Oh, no! I squeezed the
pinch-bell! They'll be on their way back,
and the house is a wreck!" cried Gormy,
panicking.

"Don't worry, Gormy," said Nana. "I've
spent two hundred years cleaning up after
myself – all it takes is a little magic. . ."

Actually, it took quite a lot of magic to put the house and garden back the way it was. Nana made her way around the house, twirling her fat finger here, *POP!*, there, *POP!*, and everywhere. And with every twirl and *POP!* something was magically repaired. From the trees, to the walls, to the grandmonster clock – it was all in a day's work for a guilty noog. She even used her magic to close the trap door in the Room of Doom! Before Gormy knew it, everything was back the way it should be.

"Nana, that was amazing!" said Gormy, his mouth agape.

"And just in time – look who's back. . ." said Mike, glancing out of the front window. A second later, Grumbor and Mogra crashed through the door.

"Gormy, my precious furball, where are you?" roared his mother, almost trampling him. "We heard the pinch-bell squeal – are you all right? Was it wolves? How many were there? What happened, Gormy?"

Gormy looked at Nana. For a moment she looked as though she was going to confess all, so he said, "Everything's fine. I, um . . . I had a *nightmare*. That's it. I had a nightmare and I was scared, so I squeezed the pinch-bell," said Gormy, sheepishly.

"You had a *nightmare*?" cried Grumbor, in disbelief. "But monsters don't have nightmares! Monsters are *in* nightmares! You can't have a nightmare, it's . . . it's just not *monstrous*!"

"Oh, leave the boy alone,

Grumbor," said Mogra. She grabbed Gormy
and hugged him so tightly that he thought

he might burst. When he got his breath
back, he breathed an enormous sigh of
relief. He hated looking so unmonstrous in
front of his father, but he was glad that, for
once, no one had got into trouble.

"Well, that's put an end to our
monsterversary," grumbled Grumbor, "and
I was just about to have my claws

buffed. . ."

"You should go back! There's still time! I promise I won't squeeze the pinch-bell again. And Nana's here to look after me, so there won't be any trouble," said Gormy.

"Oh, I don't know . . . are you sure?" said Mogra. "I mean, do you think you could cope with another night of being monstersat?"

"Definitely!" Gormy answered, with a smile.

Eleven

Lesson - five hundred and fivety - six
Nana knows Best

After a nice hot cup of sheep tea, Gormy's parents said their goodbyes and set off down Peatree Hill for the second time.

"Thanks for not telling them about the whole noog-monster thing, Gormy," said Nana. "At least now you know *why* you have to stay in your room tonight."

"Don't worry, I've learned my lesson. Nana knows best!" said Gormy, with a glint in his eye.

"Now you're getting it! Right, then, how about a few noog games to start the day?" said Nana.

"Actually, um, it's been a long night . . . and I'm very tired. I think I might go to bed for the day," said Gormy, yawning a big "look how tired I am!" yawn.

Much to Nana's surprise, Gormy headed straight for his room, yawning loudly all the way. But the second he closed the door, his yawn turned into a grin. It was a grin so full of monstrousness that it actually made Gormy's fang grow a little longer.

Of course, Gormy hadn't learned his lesson at all. He was only going to bed so he'd be wide awake by bedtime! After all, he would much rather give up another day of playing with Nana, so that he could have another night of "playing" with the Nana-monster! It had been the most monstrous night of his whole life!

Gormy wasn't even sure there were enough pages left in his **How to be a Better Monster** book to write down all the monstrous things he'd done – he'd learned how to "know his snow", nearly been eaten *and* stomped on, fallen down a trap door, parachuted out of the treehouse and managed to survive a night with a monster-eating monster! He couldn't wait to do it all over again!

Still, he didn't want to ruin his parents' monsterversary again. He would have to make it through the night *without* squeezing the pinch-bell. He took it from around his neck, put it into his Big Chest of Monstrously Excellent Things, and locked the chest tight. Then he tucked himself up in bed and waited for it to get dark.

"See you soon, Nana," said Gormy, his grin more monstrous than ever, "and remember – Gormy knows best!"

Look out for more **MONSTER** mayhem

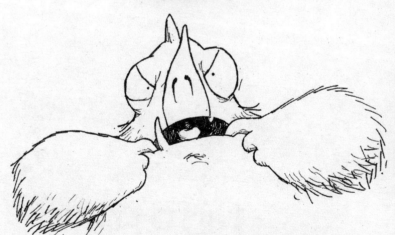

GORMY RUCKLES
MONSTER BOY

MONSTER
laughs!

GUY BASS
Illustrations by Ross Collins

GORMY RUCKLES
MONSTER Mischief

MONSTER laughs!

GUY BASS
Illustrations by Ross Collins

Gormy Ruckles

Monster Birthday

MONSTER laughs!

Guy Bass

Illustrations by Ross Collins

Charlie

If you like Gormy, why not look out for my adventures!

Meet Charlie - he's trouble!

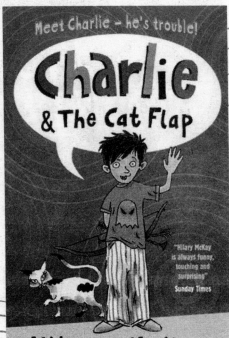

Meet Charlie - he's trouble!

Charlie & The Cat Flap

"Hilary McKay
is always funny,
touching and
surprising"
Sunday Times

Hilary McKay

Charlie and Henry are staying the
night at Charlie's house. They've made
a deal, but the night doesn't go quite
as Charlie plans. . .

Meet Charlie – he's trouble!

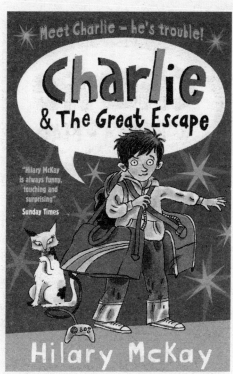

Charlie's fed up with his mean family always picking on him – so he's decided to run away. That'll show them! Now they'll be sorry!

But running away means being boringly, IMPOSSIBLY quiet…

Meet Charlie – he's trouble!

"The snow's all getting wasted! What'll we do? It will never last till after school!"

Charlie's been waiting for snow his whole life, but now it's come, everyone's trying to spoil it! Luckily, Charlie has a very clever plan to keep it safe…

Meet Charlie – he's trouble!

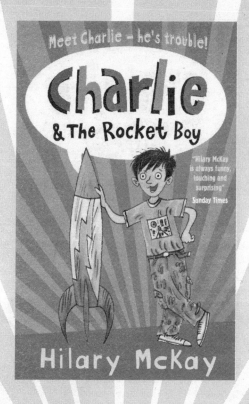

Meet Charlie – he's trouble!

Charlie & The Rocket Boy

"Hilary McKay is always funny, touching and surprising"
Sunday Times

Hilary McKay

"Zachary is a liar, liar, pants on fire!"

There's a new boy in Charlie's class. Zachary says his dad is away on a rocket but Charlie knows that's rubbish… Isn't it?

Meet Charlie – he's trouble!

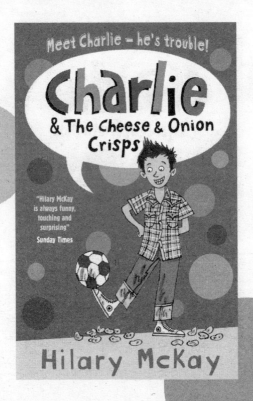

*Charlie has given up
cheese and onion crisps!*

He just hasn't been himself lately.
There's only one thing for it – the
Truly Amazing Smarties Trick!

Meet Charlie – he's trouble!

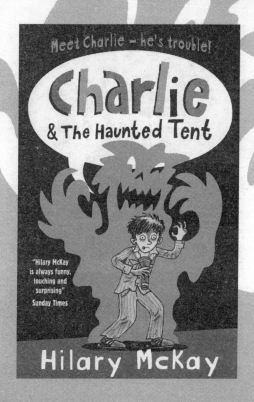

Charlie's big brother Max isn't scared of anything ... Except Aunt Emma's spooky house

At last it's Charlie's chance to be the hero. Those ghosts had better watch out!

Meet Charlie – he's trouble!

Have you met Charlie?

Along with big brother Max and best friend Henry, Charlie can't help but have the most fun, most daring, most crazy adventures ever!